D1088380

Thank you to my crocodille sisters, Arlette Dunn, Mara Irsara and Vivien Wilson for all their support.

THE CROC WHO ROCKED

LAURA CASELLA

Once upon a time,
in a very, very quiet part of the jungle...

some crocodile eggs softly hatched.
The baby crocs ran off quickly in all directions,

but one egg was hopping and **bop-dee-bopping!**

But the other animals didn't like his **snappy, snappy song** in their quiet jungle.

SNAP SNAP SNAP SNAP SNAP SNAP SNAP

Little Croc was sad.

Time passed, and little Croc became a very big croc.

His **SNAP-SNAP** song got better and much louder,

SNAP SNAP

but still no one wanted to hear it.

SHHHHHH!

Croc didn't understand why the other animals disliked his happy
SNAPPY-SNAPPY song. He wished he could sing
 a different song, like the birds that sometimes
cleaned crocodiles' teeth.

He slipped sadly again into the water, wondering if he would ever sing in the jungle
for all the animals.

Later, two birds landed on his tail.
They were looking for a croc so
they could clean its teeth
and eat the food stuck in them.

Croc was very happy to see them.

He told them how sad and lonely he was.

The two birds felt sorry for him.

They agreed to teach him how to tweet

in exchange for some food.

Day after day, the birds taught him their **tweety** song.

Night after night, he practised and practised.

Croc was happy.

He had finally learned to tweet a sweet-sounding song.

His next challenge was to sing it to all the other animals.

Croc returned to the jungle.
He sang his new **tweet-tweet** song,
and to his surprise...

Tweet
Doo Boom Baby Tweet Boom Pow

Uh Uh Baby Uhhh Uh

Hiss Hiss Baby Hisssss

Croak Baby Croak Croak

Croc was having so much fun that he forgot to tweet.

SNAP Tweet SNAP Baby Tweet SNAP

His jaws banged together, and before he could stop himself, out came a very loud

SNAP Tweet Baby Tweet SNAP

SNAP

SNAP

The animals went quiet, looked at each other in fear .... and ran away

Tweet SNAP SNAP SNAP SNAP BABY SNAP

Croc returned alone to the river, singing sadly to himself. His loud, snappy song echoed over the water. Long, sharp noses and bulging eyes appeared on the surface.

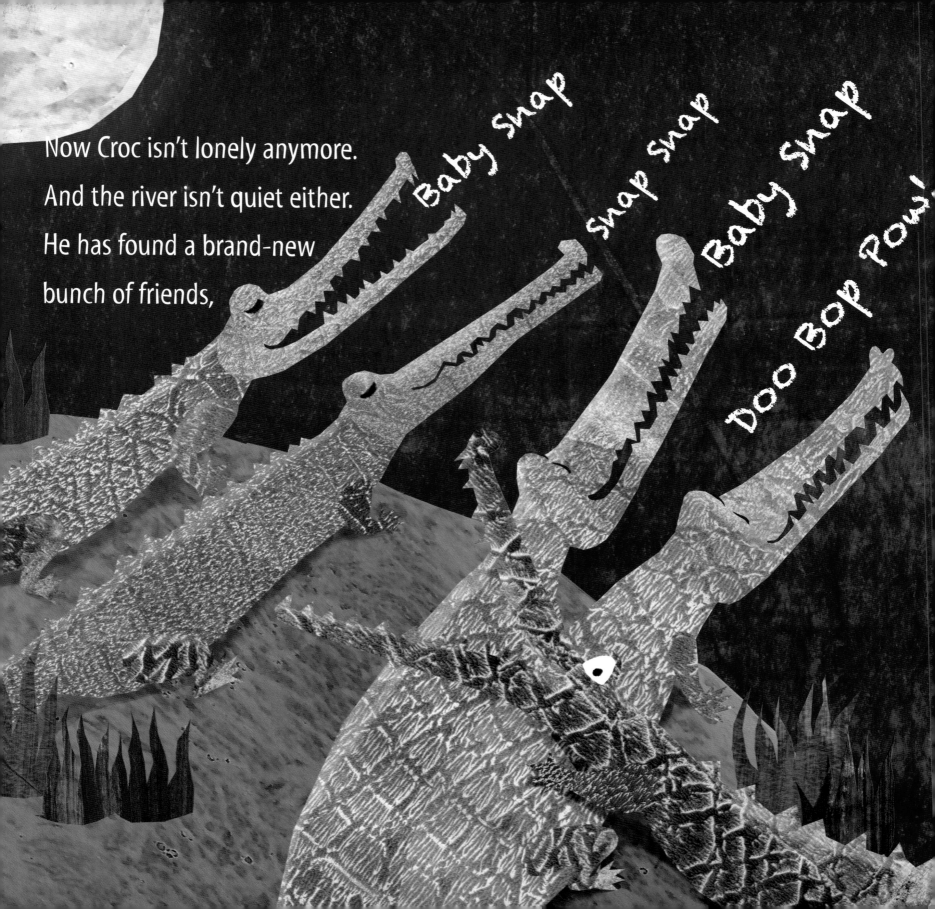

Now Croc isn't lonely anymore.
And the river isn't quiet either.
He has found a brand-new
bunch of friends,

Baby Snap

Snap Snap

Baby Snap

Doo Bop Pow!

Tweet Baby Tweet Snap Snap Doo Wop Pow Tweet Snap Snap Doo Be Be Bop

..and they sing his
special song
all night long.

Starfish Bay® Children's Books
An imprint of Starfish Bay Publishing
www.starfishbaypublishing.com

THE CROC WHO ROCKED

© Laura Casella, 2018
ISBN 978-1-76036-052-8
First Published 2018
Printed in China by Toppan Leefung Printing (Shanghai) Co., Ltd.
No. 106 Qingda Road, Pudong, New Area, Shanghai, 201201, China

Laura Casella was born in Rome. She obtained a BA in Illustration

from the Institute of European Design. In 1995, her work

was selected at the Children's Book Fair in Bologna for her non-fiction project Middle Ages.

In 1996, she moved to London, where she worked as a graphic/web designer also using

her illustration skills. She recently graduated from Anglia

Ruskin in Cambridge with a MA in Children's Book Illustration.

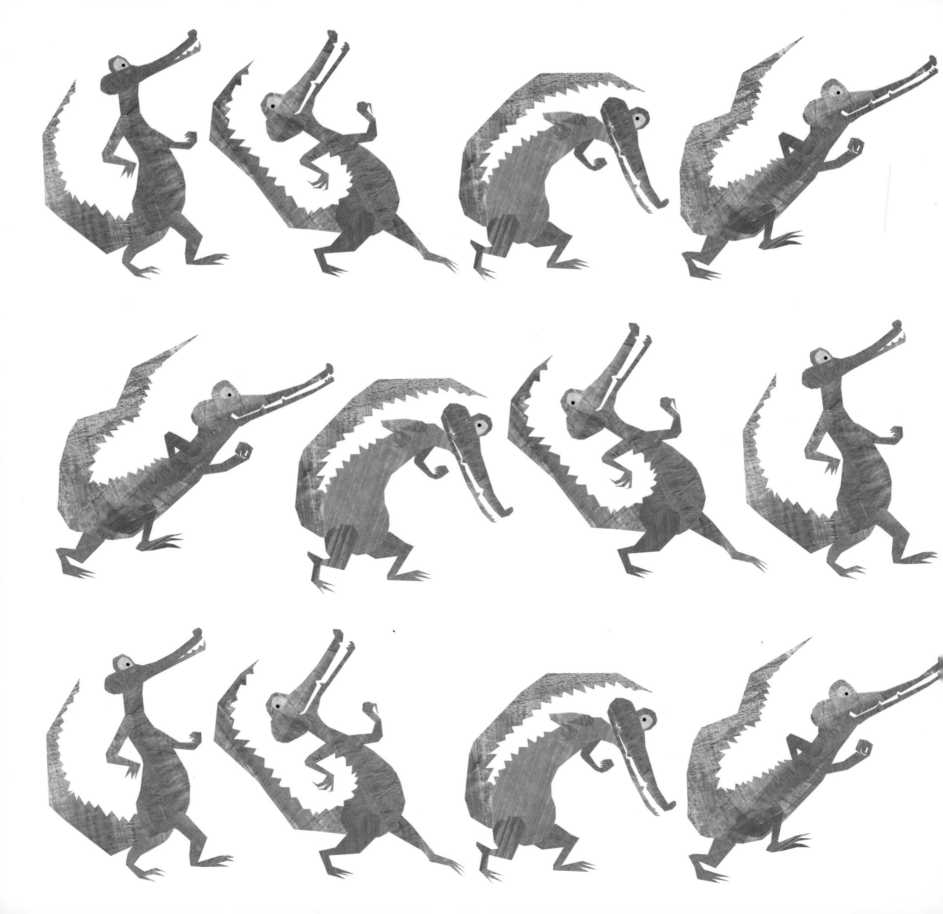